Second Death

By Peter Frost David

Lara's Prologue

This is Jake's journal. It's classified because of where Jake was when he wrote it. I can't tell you much about how he smuggled it up because I don't want to make it harder for him to send information to me in the future. Except for changing names and a few other details to protect the identities of the living and the dead, this is exactly what my husband wrote.

- Lara

Chapter 1

Are You Evil?

January 16

Recall the coyote and roadrunner cartoon. Was the coyote evil?

Are you evil?

Which is worse: endless pain or endless boredom?

Which would you prefer: a painless early death or a long life of suffering?

Have you ever prayed for something horrible to happen to another person?

Suppose the universe really is "turtles all the way down." How would knowledge of this cosmic truth affect your career choices?

If Jesus was drafted into the US Army, what rank would he rise to?

Would you sacrifice your life to save a loved one from agonizing pain?

And so on. For two hours. I sat on a stool in an empty chamber. The questions were read to me through a speaker and I answered to a mirrored wall.

I passed the interview.

Twenty of us showed up for the intake interview. Men and women, active duty and civilian, who each thought it was a good idea to apply for a six-month post with quadruple hazard pay. In other words, twenty government workers whose financial problems were serious enough to drive them to an ultra-high-risk post for a few extra bucks.

We chatted and compared notes in the waiting room. All of us had applied for the same job: Refugee Operation Manager. Nobody but me had experience in humanitarian aid or refugee management. The group was mostly a mixture of consular officers from State, civil affairs folks from DoD, and health officers from the Centers for Disease Control.

We had a few things in common, though. We all had security clearances. And we were all desperate to earn that hazard pay. Some of us had children in college. Some had a sick relative. Some had fallen far behind in their bills. I had all three of those burdens. My daughter Cara had just started college and Lara's multiple sclerosis got bad enough that she had to quit her job. On top of that, our mortgage was crushing us financially. I *had* to take this post.

Whatever qualities they were probing for with their weirdo questions must be rare. After waiting for two hours, fifteen folks were told that they "lacked the unique worldview required for this post." Those lacking the appropriate perspective on life or whatever were thanked for their time and sent home.

The five of us who were "lucky" enough to possess the required mental framework to handle this post got to stick around in the waiting area for another two hours. We passed the time by eyeing each other suspiciously, wondering what kind of people these were to have passed this test. I mean, I know *I'm* cool, but anyone *else* who passed that test had to have multiple interacting personality disorders.

The same staffer who sent the rejected candidates home finally returned pushing a cart loaded with food service trays and a stack of folded grey clothing. She apologized for making us wait. Then told us that the food was a specially-prepared high-calorie and high-protein stew. "Eat as much of it as you can and then change into the uniforms. When you're done eating and in uniform, I'll escort you to the descent chamber."

I asked her what a descent chamber was. Her answer was terse: "You'll receive a full mission briefing *after* descent. For now, please just eat and suit up."

I asked her why we couldn't get a mission briefing now, so we knew what we were getting into.

She stood up straight and took a deep breath. When she spoke, she spoke carefully — I was getting the pre-canned spiel. "We have found, through evidence-based analyses, that briefing candidates *after* descent optimizes our attrition rate."

"Oh, I get it!" My fellow selectee, a woman I now knew as Karen, interrupted. "Everyone quits if you tell them what's up before they get there. Nice."

The strain in the staffer's smile told us that Karen had hit the nail on the head. "If all goes well, you'll be at post and briefed within the next ninety minutes."

Ninety minutes? We were in friggin' Maryland. I had no idea how we could get anywhere in the world dangerous enough to rate quadruple hazard pay in ninety minutes.

The stew was thick and chewy. Taste and edibility were sacrificed at the altar of protein content and calorie count.

We joked about the food as we got into uniform. "Quadruple hazard pay won't be enough if they make us eat this at every meal!" Ha ha.

There were no changing rooms, so we took turns ducking into the bathroom to put on our uniforms. My grey uniform fit loosely. Aside from the American flag patch on the shoulders, it bore no insignias or any other markings. I looked more like a janitor than a ... what? What was I supposed to be doing in this job? The job announcement was for a Refugee Operations Manager. But in my 20 years in humanitarian aid, I never had to wear unmarked battle fatigues to work.

The descent chamber, whatever that was, apparently existed deep under the same building where we had our intake interviews. The five of us, now wearing our shabby, moondust-grey military fatigues, were led through long hallways and down broad stairwells. As we made our way deeper into the facility, I noticed a subtle change in the way the security was organized.

In the interview area, building security was tight, but still consisted of the usual stuff designed to keep unauthorized people out. Access was controlled by security vestibules with entry/exit interlocks, doors that opened only when the security officer behind them buzzed you in, and that sort of thing. But deep in the facility everything changed. The reinforced doors, the vestibules, and the turnstiles and mantrap portals were all organized to carefully control *exit*, not entry.

The signs posted next to the doors we passed were also unsettling: Portal Operations, Hospice Care, Advanced Theology & Ethics, Cartography. Finally, the hallway ended at a huge metal door labeled *Descent*.

Our escort turned to us. "One of the major selection criteria for this post is an ability to follow instructions. Now is the time to exercise your above-average instruction-following skills. Listen carefully."

We listened very carefully.

"In a moment I will open this door. We will enter a large interior space, about the size of a gymnasium. I will close this door as soon as we are all inside. Two shapes are painted on the floor exactly two-hundred fifteen feet from this door: a red circle and a blue square. Walk into the red circle. If, at any time, you choose not to continue to your post, you may walk to the blue square. If you enter the blue square, you will be debriefed and sent home. A man at a desk near the red circle will call you forward one at a time to give you your descent instructions and fare. After you receive your descent instructions and fare you will have one last chance to move to the blue square. Once you enter the portal, you will not be able to leave until your ascent, six months from now."

She opened the door. We stepped into the dim space beyond.

I spent *maybe* four minutes in the descent chamber. Those four minutes completely unraveled my understanding of the universe. I thought the crazy questions they asked at my interview – *Jesus in the US Army? Endless pain vs. endless boredom?* – were just a verbal Rorschach test to see what

9

I'd say. I didn't think they were asking me questions about actual, concrete situations.

We shuffled through the door and looked around with dumb, open-mouthed expressions. For five or ten seconds, my brain produced no conscious, coherent thoughts. There was too much information to assimilate. When my scattered mental activity finally coalesced into something that could be considered a thought, it was a dumb one. I thought about my neighbor when I was growing up: Kenny Timmerman.

I worked hard in high school, and graduated third in my class. My senior year I took AP chemistry and AP physics at the same time. The workload was insane. My neighbor Kenny, on the other hand, put his teenage effort into being the best metal-head-slacker that he could be. He wore a black leather jacket *every day*, no matter what the weather. He had decorated the jacket himself – it was adorned with patches featuring upside down crosses and what I assume were the names of hyper-obscure metal bands written in nearly-unreadably ornate gothic letters. On the back, Kenny had set silver studs in the shape of a pentagram – an upside-down star inside a circle.

Whenever I saw Kenny – at the bus stop or the mall – I would indulge in thoughts about how much better-off I would eventually be than Kenny, due to my diligent investment in my studies, and my work ethic. What I saw in that huge dark room dug into the Maryland bedrock annihilated that line of thinking.

Kenny, who sacrificed his academic studies to instead focus on perfecting his unique combination of screaming, sticking out his tongue, and making the metal-goat-devil sign with his thumbs and pinkies, had come far, *far* closer to uncovering the true reality than I had with my studies of science. In the Descent Chamber, I realized that chemistry and physics were silly diversions to keep mankind from approaching the real truth of the universe.

Although the descent chamber was a simple rectangular space, it clearly had a front and back. We entered through a door on the right side of the room. To our left, the rear of the chamber, was a huge, hundred-foot-long window of glass. The well-lit space behind the glass was filled with rows of men and women sitting behind desks laden with computer monitors, phones, and other electronic gear. Houston space-control from the 1969 Apollo program, with updated computers and screens.

Most of the floor was used to form what I can only describe as a defensive line. Pillboxes and concrete barriers were installed in patterns reminiscent of the arrangement of cannons in fifteenth-century fortifications. Dozens – maybe hundreds – of grey-fatigued soldiers were manning these positions. Rifles, rocket launchers, every kind of weapon an infantry regiment might need were on display. Concrete towers built against the walls held anti-aircraft cannons. All this weaponry was trained on the front of the room.

The front wall validated Kenny Timmerman's adolescence. It validated the Spanish Inquisition. It validated Tipper Gore's stance on music censorship. It validated the Salem Witch Trials.

Mounted on the wall in the front of the room was a fifty-foot-tall, glowing-red star inscribed in a circle. A pentagram. The center of the star was a perfectly pentagonal black pit leading into the wall.

"Walk to the red circle." The words were directed at me, but I didn't walk anywhere. My mind was too jammed to process the staffer's instructions. "*Sir*. Please walk to the red circle."

I followed her pointing finger. A bright red circle, large enough to hold fifty people, was painted on the floor directly in front of the pentagram. I looked around in near-panic for the blue square. I found it near the rear of the chamber.

"Sir. Please walk to the red circle."

I started walking. My legs shook, but I kept my balance. I glanced behind me. Two of my fellow "chosen ones" had followed me. But an older man I only knew as Kent was running towards the blue square.

I had a better view of the pentagram from inside the red circle. The pentagram was traced out by thick metal wires glowing red from heat. It looked like an enormous, Satanic, electric stove burner. From the vantage point of the red circle, I could perceive some of the details of the pentagram's construction. The wall it was mounted on was made of metal panels. I could see the seams between the panels and the heads of the bolts that held them in place. Electrical conduit was routed to the vertices of the star. Small, high-voltage warning signs, and stickers that said *Portal-Certified Personnel Only* were affixed to the metal surface at regular intervals. The black pentagonal hole leading into the wall remained featureless, however. It was a perfectly formed, perfectly black hole, with no features visible inside.

A rolling metal staircase was pushed against the glowing star, giving access to the pentagonal tunnel in the center. A man with a crew cut sat behind a desk at the base of the stairs. He wore a white, short-sleeved, button-up shirt and a black tie. Two or three pens poked out of his shirt pocket. He removed his glasses and cleaned them with a small cloth as our group, now only four, arrived in the circle. The desk was as ordinary a desk as they make – the same grey-painted steel desk found at the head of every public-school classroom in the country.

The man at the desk read out our names from a stack of paperwork. "Bolens!" He shouted to be heard clearly from the desk, fifty feet from our red circle.

"He's in the blue square!" The woman next to me apparently had learned Kent's last name.

The man at the desk put the folder down and picked up another. "Clark!"

The woman who knew Kent's last name left the circle and slowly walked to the desk. She spoke with the man for a minute, then turned and walked back to us. "No damn way," she said as walked past, heading to the blue square.

"Fenders!"

The middle-aged man who introduced himself as Charles when we met this morning, trudged to the desk. He spoke to mister shirt-and-tie for a minute, zipped something into the breast pocket of his grey uniform, then dutifully climbed the stairs. Charles reached the top of the stairs, took a last look behind him, and stepped into the black hole.

"Conner!"

I took a deep breath and walked out of the red circle, towards the desk and the looming pentagram behind it. The heat from the glowing red wires grew noticeably with each step towards the desk.

I focused on desk-man's face. A thin, fifty-something guy with a greying flat-top. A shirt and tie out of the 1950s. He looked bored. Another day at the office. He handed me two heavy silver coins the size of casino chips and said "zip these into your breast pocket. Do not remove them or unzip your pocket." He spoke clearly and deliberately, like he was reading someone the instructions for defusing a bomb.

"Climb the stairs, enter the tunnel, and walk forward," he continued in the same deliberate tone. "Do not speak the names of the dead. Do not pray. Say yes if you understand these instructions."

"Yes." I understood *what* to do. But *why*? Don't *pray*?

"Enter the tunnel."

I climbed the steps and entered the tunnel.

Chapter 2

The Boatman

January 16 (continued)

The interior of the tunnel was completely dark. I couldn't tell if my eyes were open or shut. I heard the faint footsteps of Charles, the man who entered before me, and tried to follow him. Without any visual reference, my sense of balance went loopy. I sensed I was walking downhill. Then uphill. Then I had a sickening twisting sensation and I couldn't shake the feeling that I was walking on the walls and the ceiling. Gravity snapped back into its usual relationship with my feet the instant I saw the faint light at the end. I jogged towards it, in a hurry to get out.

We exited the tunnel through an irregular, jagged gash in the side of an enormous boulder. I kept walking about fifty feet more once I exited, desperate to get far away from the awful darkness of the tunnel. The boulder that was the terminus of the pentagram's central portal sat, half buried, on a desolate, rocky plain. The sky was black, with no moon and no stars. A dim, diffuse light directly overhead illuminated the bleak landscape.

A sign, painted in the green and white of standard US highway signs, was planted directly in front of the tunnel exit. It said:

FOLLOW THE LIGHTED PATH TO THE BOATMAN

DO NOT SPEAK THE NAMES OF THE DEAD

DO NOT PRAY

The candidate behind me, the thirty-something Karen, evidently chose to enter the portal too and emerged behind me a few seconds later. Of the twenty of us that started this morning, only three of us made it this far. We milled around at the end of the tunnel for a minute, trying to keep from falling into a blind panic. That's what I was doing, anyway. I tried to joke around to make myself feel better. I said, "I guess we're not in Maryland anymore." Nobody laughed. I didn't feel better.

A line of blinking LEDs on stakes wound into the dismal landscape. This was obviously the "LIGHTED PATH" in the instructions on the sign.

We silently followed the line of lights for about a kilometer. I peered into the gloom to try to learn something about our environment. There were no trees. There was no vegetation of any kind. I didn't see insects or birds or any sign of animal life. Nothing but grey boulders, grey rocks, and grey dirt.

Dim and indistinct features appeared in the distance and gradually became clear as we continued to follow the line of lights. A black streak across the horizon resolved itself into a wide, slowly moving river. The faint constellation of lights at the end of the trail turned into a small complex of tents and utility lights on poles powered by a portable generator. Crates of various sizes were stacked in irregular piles inside the lighted area.

That's where I met the dead Marine. He had clearly been killed by the foot-long piece of shrapnel that protruded from his chest. I was okay with the horrible wound – I can handle blood – but I lost it when he asked me for a cigarette.

"Mister, you got a smoke?" He was sitting on a short stack of crates. His uniform was a drab green color, with an old-style fit and canvas boots — a uniform from decades before the modern pixelated camo pattern became standard. "USMC" was stenciled on the chest pocket of his uniform.

The Marine hopped off the crates. His skin was as grey as the ground, and his eyes were as dark as the black sky. He stepped onto the trail in front of me. "I'm talkin' to you. You got a smoke?"

My heart began pounding and I felt dizzy. My mouth and my brain disconnected from each other – I couldn't put my thoughts into words. I jumped back and fell onto the trail behind me. I screamed.

The Marine shook his head in disapproval. "I guess that's a no. Thanks."

"Corporal, back to your post!"

A sergeant stormed out of one of the tents that were erected in the circle of battery-powered light. He appeared to be alive – his skin looked as if blood was pumping underneath it. His eyes were the eyes of a living person. He wore the same grey uniform that we did, but his bore insignia of rank: three stripes up and two down. I made a mental note to myself: now that I'm tangled up in a military operation, I really need to learn about ranks.

"I told you," The living Sergeant continued berating the dead Marine, "nobody down here smokes! We screen out smokers from candidates."

The dead Marine ambled off to the edge of the pool of light mumbling something about not having had a cigarette for eighty years. The Sergeant waited until we had gathered under the lights. The name "Gibson" was embroidered on his shirt.

"Ladies and gentlemen. You are about to take a short boat ride. I hope you all still have the silver coins you were given prior to descent." He spoke with the loud and ironically-cheery cadence of a drill instructor.

He waited for the general murmuring of affirmation to die out.

"Very good. I'm going to ask each of you to take some gear with you."

"Some gear" turned out to be an eighty-pound pack for each of us. There were fifty enormous rucksacks in the tent, each one stuffed to the limit with gear. Sergeant Gibson pointed me to the pack he wanted me to carry. I unrolled the top and peeked inside. It was full of bullets. They weren't even in boxes. It was just a pack full of eighty pounds of loose bullets.

We helped each other strap on the brutally-heavy packs. Then the dead Corporal and living Sergeant Gibson escorted us down the short segment of trail from the supply camp to the river bank.

The trail delivered us onto a small beach of coarse grey pebbles. From here, the river took on the color of the sky, and looked more like a wide, lazy flow of black ink than of water.

Charles, Karen, and I waited on the bank, wobbling under the weight of our packs. The dead Marine and Sergeant Gibson stood back, watched us, watched the river, and watched the shore.

Gibson checked his watch and announced, "About five minutes until he comes. Listen up! I know you haven't been briefed in yet, so a lot of these instructions may seem ... unusual. Just do what I say and you'll be fine."

Charles, Karen, and I once again got ready to apply our advanced instruction-following skills.

"Board the boat one at a time. Keep your weight low and stay in the center of the boat. Once you're underway, keep your arms inside the boat. Do not touch the water. Do not speak to the boatman."

"Look!"

Charles pointed to the river. The boatman was coming.

The boat was a few hundred meters from the shore. We all squinted to make out the details of the watercraft and its pilot. From the distance, it looked a bit like a person on a stand-up paddleboard.

The boat slowly approached the shore and it became apparent that it wasn't a stand-up paddleboard. It looked more like a man standing in a canoe, or in a Venetian gondola. The closer the boat got, the more wrong it looked. The boat was too small. No, that wasn't it. The boat was a good thirty feet long. The problem was that the boatman was enormous. He was taller than the Tallest Man in the World statue in the lobby of every *Ripley's Believe It or Not* museum. He was skinnier too. The boat came closer still. The boatman was an enormously tall haggard old man, dressed in black rags. He clutched the sculling oar with skeletal fingers.

"Shit," Charles said. He crossed himself.

"What the fuck did you just do!" Gibson screamed at Charles. "Did you just fucking CROSS yourself? What don't you understand about 'Don't Pray!' It's a simple fucking instruction!"

"I, it's just a habit. I didn't even say anything."

"Oh shit, here we go," the dead Corporal said. He jumped onto a boulder and began scanning the horizon. Gibson unslung his rifle and moved to the base of the boulder.

"Listen people! The Corporal and I are going to have our hands full in a moment. No matter what happens on this beach, get in the fucking boat. Get in as fast as you can and get off this beach!"

"I see two." The Marine reported. "200 yards out. It looks like a burner and a biter ... Make that three. One burner and two biters."

"Where are they?" Gibson asked.

"At the base of that boulder."

Gibson fired three shots in the direction the Marine pointed.

"Not that boulder, the closer one. Just give me the rifle, sergeant."

"You know the rules." Gibson fired again.

"You missed. They've stopped advancing."

I scanned the terrain and thought I saw the boulder the Corporal was talking about. I didn't see anything near it. Neither did anyone else, apparently. "What are you shooting at?" Karen shouted.

"You can't see them. The living can't see them," Gibson shouted back.

"See what?!" I asked.

The Corporal answered me. "The demons. Only the dead can see them."

Gibson fired three more shots. "Missed again," the Marine grumbled. Then he turned his dead black eyes to me. "You can't see them, but they'll kill you plenty dead." He turned back to the landscape. "They're advancing. Fire again." Gibson fired four more rounds towards the boulder. "The burner is down. Biters stopped advancing."

This was my first actual, live-fire, someone's-going-to-die gunfight. My heart began beating so hard it hurt. The surge of adrenaline was so powerful I felt like my eyes were going to pop out of my head. My body was ramped up for action, but I had no idea what to actually do. I didn't have a gun to shoot at anything. Even if I did, I didn't see what the threat was. *Burners*? *Biters*? What the hell was the dead Marine talking about?

I decided to lie down. *Hit the deck*, isn't that what soldier-types say when there's *incoming*? Hitting the deck with an eighty-pound pack full of bullets is pretty tricky. I dropped to a crouch but the inertia from the pack kept moving me downwards. I landed on my side, bruising my hip and scraping a decent amount of skin off my forearm.

Once on the ground, on the *deck*, I realized that the pack was so heavy I could barely move. I felt trapped instead of safe. Panic set in and I struggled to stand back up. I got as far as pushing myself onto my knees before I was so out-of-breath that I had to take a break. Gibson fired a long salvo of shots towards whatever invisible things were out there. I closed my eyes, squeezing out a few tears.

Then another layer of terror enveloped me. The fear from the gun battle with whatever was hunting us faded to almost nothing as a new horror flooded my mind. The boatman was near.

The boat crunched against the gravelly riverbank behind us. I was almost too scared to turn around to look at him. It's not that I was afraid of what I'd see. I was terrified of the boatman seeing *me*. I felt his presence behind me. I somehow knew he was looking at us. Contemplating us. Applying his intelligence and dark personality to the problem of knowing who we were, and what our lives stood for.

Against my will, my mind contemplated ancient, decrepit things. Rotting coffins. Forgotten tombs in the basements of ancient churches. Bleached bones on a desiccated desert floor. My mind resonated with the boatman's, and these were the thoughts that leaked into my head from his.

I sensed joy in the boatman as well – the joy of being part of the machinery of all human death. He was the transporter of the souls of the damned. I didn't want that thing to know me. To look at me. To think about me.

"Biters advancing again," the Corporal reported.

"Get in the damn boat, people!" Gibson shouted before firing again.

I somehow rose from my knees to my feet, and found myself looking straight into the eyes of the boatman. Clouds of deep, dim colors swirled in his irises. The skin of his face was wrinkled. No, that's not even the right word. Furrowed. Folded. His skin looked like the bark of a long-dead tree, or parched earth. But his eyes were young. Energetic. Eager. That's the best way to describe them. He was eager to take the dead. After the countless millennia of doing his job, he still deeply craved the dead.

Then he *spoke my name*. He pointed to me and said "Jake Conner." His voice was old and gravely, but still full of strength and authority. And a delighted energy.

I felt a tickle in my shirt pocket. The boatman opened his hand to show me two silver coins in his palm. I touched the pocket where I had safely zipped away the coins I was given in the descent chamber. The pocket was empty. The boatman gestured to the boat and I got on.

The boat was roughly constructed from wood that was black with age. The gunwalls and deck were worn smooth from, I assume, the countless passengers it had transported. Despite my uncoordinated scramble into the boat and the eighty-pound pack I wore, the boat barely rocked when I found my seat.

Even though I was averting my gaze by staring directly at the deck, I somehow knew that he stopped contemplating me. He said the next name. "Karen Volks."

I turned to watch Karen board the boat. Behind her, Charles waited impatiently on the bank, flinching each time Gibson fired at his unseen targets. Charles turned his head as if he heard a noise behind him. Then he flew into the air like he was struck by an invisible car from behind. A long splash of blood burst from his chest and traced his twisting arc through the air. He crumpled into a heap on the ground.

"Behind us!" the Marine shouted.

Gibson spun around and fired a burst into the space above Charles' body.

"It's running," the Corporal reported. Gibson fired again. "It's gone!" he shouted. "Cease fire!"

The Marine turned back to the original group of demons. "Biters advancing." Gibson fired another burst. "They've stopped."

Charles sat up. His face was grey and his eyes were black. "I'm dead," he said calmly. Factually. "I felt myself die. I'm dead now."

"No!" I shouted. "You're not dead. Just stay still. We'll get help."

"He's fucking dead," the Marine shouted. "Now everyone get on the boat!"

I screamed at the Marine. "He's sitting up and talking. He's still alive."

"You don't know shit!" the Marine shouted back. "Look at the boatman!"

I carefully turned to look at the ancient entity, ready to turn away instantly if he was looking at me. But the boatman was looking at Charles. He smiled manically, seemingly over-the-moon happy about Charles' apparent death. He held out his hand, gesturing Charles onto the boat. "Charles Kittering."

Charles rose up and dusted himself off. Wet, bloody stains the size of dinner plates grew from the wounds in his back and his chest. "I'm dead. I felt life leave me," he repeated.

"Wait!" Gibson turned away from his invisible targets. He approached Charles and blocked his path to the boat. He unzipped the pocket on Charles' uniform and took out the silver coins. "No need to waste a fare," he said grimly. "The boatman transports the dead for free."

Gibson hoisted Charles' bloodstained pack onto his shoulders. "Sorry about this. But we have to get these supplies across the river."

Charles glumly crawled into the boat, leaving a trail of blood on the seats and deck.

The boatman pushed us off the beach and into the black water of the river.

The ride across the river was endless. Behind me stood the boatman, methodically working the sculling oar, propelling us inevitably forward. Karen was in front of me, silent and still. Charles sat in front of Karen, moaning and holding his hands to his chest. Gibson's instruction to avoid talking to the boatman was completely unnecessary. I can't imagine anyone wanting to be the subject of the boatman's attention for a millisecond longer than they had to.

I tried to offer Charles encouragement. "You'll be okay. You're just in shock from your wound. We'll get help on the other side of the river."

Charles didn't respond. The gunshots from the shore faded away. Or maybe Gibson stopped firing. There was no turbulence and soon the only sound was the soft sloshing of water against the hull.

The shore ahead was a blurry grey smear between the black river and the black sky. We moved forward at the boatman's slow, deliberate speed and eventually the blurry grey smear became another shore. Another desolate grey moonscape of gravel and boulders. Low, jagged hills rose in the distance a few kilometers away from the river.

A dim constellation of lights was visible directly ahead. The boatman drove us forward and the lights grew brighter and seemed to multiply. Eventually the organization of the lights became clear. I could see a fence line, floodlights illuminating a city of tents, and streetlights marking broad avenues between the tents. It was a small town. A small outpost of the living on the far side of the river.

A sign on the bank – also painted in the standard green and white of the US road system – said:

FORT KAIZEN

(HELL)

Chapter 3

37.9% Of People Go To Hell when they Die

January 16 (continued)

Thanks to a classified and well-funded scientific research program, we know that 37.9% of people go to Hell when they die. We also know that when they get there, they will encounter a physical environment with a gravitational force only 97% of the Earth's and an atmosphere with 2% greater oxygen content. Our mission briefing pointed out that, due to the non-standard gravity and the greater atmospheric density, it's crucial to use the updated artillery tables when putting indirect fire on longer range targets.

The mission briefing included many more fascinating facts and helpful tips about Hell. For example, researchers have documented three species of lichen that grow on the rocks as far as 10 kilometers from the river. We know, down to the milligram, the minimum mass of silver the boatman requires to transport one living person across that river, and we know the maximum weight of gear personnel can carry before the boatman refuses to serve them. We know not to speak the names of the dead when we're visiting Hell, and we've learned how dangerous it can be to pray while we're there.

Most importantly, we know that Satan exists and that he is a threat to the national security of the United States of America. Our mission is to find him and kill him.

There are two ways to get into Hell. The first is straightforward and obvious: A) be in that special 37.9% and B) die. The second way relies on a combination of cutting-edge science and state-of-the-art theology. Our mission briefing touched on the topic of this second, more elaborate, method of visiting Hell.

Eight years ago, a bizarre laboratory accident at Lawrence Livermore National Laboratories revealed a method to visit Hell *without* dying first, and without the requirement that your soul be in that lucky 37.9%. Who would've guessed that if you pass a sufficiently intense beam of positrons through the amygdala of a person at the instant of their death, *and* that person happens to be in the Hell-bound 37.9% of humans, *and* this process happens to occur in an electromagnetically isolated chamber, then you will open a small and unstable portal to the "arrivals" side of the river Styx?

This portal can be stabilized and expanded through precise thermal control. Interestingly, when you solve the differential equations for heat flow surrounding the portal, you find that the ideal shape of the stabilizing heating elements to surround the portal is a star inside a circle – a pentagram.

All this information was delivered through a PowerPoint presentation in Fort Kaizen's dining tent given by Fort Kaizen's XO, Major Williams. I know I should have had a more profound or transcendent reaction to being told some of the deepest and most classified secrets of the universe. But due to being overwhelmed and exhausted, I was mostly just pissed that I was receiving this theologically and cosmically mind-blowing shit through a PowerPoint presentation. This stuff should have been written in an ancient scroll or carved into a meteorite or something.

Karen interrupted the Major. "But where *are* we? Is this another planet? Are we underground on Earth?"

"This has only been a military operation for the past twenty-four months," the Major answered. "Prior to that, Hell was the subject of purely scientific expeditions. Between fighting off demons and interviewing the dead, the researchers on those expeditions managed to make a few observations. To the extent that we can measure it, the terrain that surrounds us exists on a perfectly flat surface, without any of the concavity or convexity that would come from being on the surface or interior of a planet. Assuming we can trust the measurements from our lasers and radars, we know that this surface extends *at least* seventy thousand miles in every direction from here. There is no detectable Coriolis force – we are not on something that is rotating. We are not on Earth. Or any other kind of object that we know of."

Karen interrupted again. "That's not possible. Gravity would –"

"Look – I have a Master's degree in mechanical engineering. I took three semesters of physics. When I ascend home in a few months, I'm going to open up all my old physics texts, lay them on the floor and take a big fat shit on them. That's how much our supposed understanding of the universe is worth. I assume that one day, someone smarter than me will come up with a theory that makes sense of all of this. In the meantime, I'm just going to work with what we know, and adapt as we continue to learn."

Karen looked like she was going to say something in response, but at that moment a corpse entered the tent carrying a stack of oil paintings. Like Charles and the Marine on the other side of the river, her skin was grey and her eyes were black. Unlike Charles and the Marine, she must have died a non-violent death in her old age, as she appeared to be a completely intact older woman. The Major happily greeted the corpse and shook her hand.

"I'd like to introduce you to the late misses B."

The corpse turned to us. "Bonjour."

"Mrs. B. has been wandering Hell since her death in 1899. In life, she was a prolific artist, known for her artistic realism and her depictions of animals." The Major beamed at her.

"Thank you," B. said in French-accented English. I have spent more than a century here, wandering the landscape and observing the demons that inhabit it. I was lucky to make contact with your military force, and I am grateful that they provided me with oils, brushes, and canvases to paint images of what I have seen."

Karen again, "we have an artist-in-residence here?"

"Oui. The living cannot see the demons. Neither can your cameras."

"We get a little bit of detection on FLIR," the Major added, "and GMTI sort-of works here, but ours is down now." Karen nodded as if she understood what the Major was talking about. I just nodded and took a mental note of the Major's main point — technology doesn't really help us down here. "So, we've adapted. We gather intel with oils and canvas."

B. set her canvases down on one of the dining facility's folding chairs.

"There are many, many different types of demons," she explained. "In fact, every demon is different. A demon's form and even its personality depend on the bloodlines it has consumed."

"Uh – bloodlines?" Karen asked.

I also had a question. "Consumed?"

The Major responded to both of us. "Demons search for dead who are related – parents and children, grandparents and great-grandparents. They eat families. The more generations, the greater the power the demon acquires.

That's why we don't speak the names of the dead here. We don't want to leak personally identifiable information."

Mrs. B. handed one of her canvases to the Major, who displayed it to us.

The painting depicted a muscular humanoid, bristling with spikes. It's eyes glowed red and its mouth was open wide, displaying rows of fangs. "A lot of the low-level demons look kind of like this. We call this kind a biter," the Major said. "I'll let you figure out why."

"That looks like the one that killed me," Charles said. "I saw it after it killed me."

"Another common demon," B. continued, "is a creature of fire."

The next painting showed another muscular, humanoid shaped creature, completely consumed by flames. "A burner. We can detect these at nearly 200 meters with thermal sensors," the Major cheerfully added.

The next painting was of a black, tentacled creature. Human-like eyes dotted its body, which was shaped more-or-less like a human brain. "Some demons see and know all," she said.

The old-lady-corpse-artist had come into the employment of the US military recently. She only had one more canvas to show us. It was an incomplete work in progress. On it, pencil lines sketched the outlines of a vicious, horned, clawed monstrosity exhaling lightning. The Major continued with his commentary "Fortunately, these are very rare."

The Major handed the four canvases back to the corpse, and thanked her for her presentation. She shuffled out of the mess tent.

"Major, I have a question," Charles said. He sounded depressed. "What's this feeling inside of me? There's a sensation. Like a tiny dancing light in my chest. I feel pain when I focus on it."

The major spun a chair around and sat on it backwards, resting his arms on the backrest. "Charles. I'm sorry that you died today. I have to tell you a few things about death."

"First of all, even though you are dead, you are still actively employed by the United States Government. You are still obligated to respect the nondisclosure agreement you signed when you received your security clearance. Your clearance will remain active until you no longer have a role to play in our mission. Your salary will continue to be paid, but it will be dispersed in accordance with your will. I hope you had one, or it'll be tied up in probate forever."

Charles somehow managed to look even more grim. Apparently, in Hell, not even death can spare you from the banal, day-to-day bullshit that the universe delivers.

"We employ many dead here. We call them *local hires*." The Major smiled, then frowned when nobody else did.

"Some of our local hires are dead servicemen, killed in action. We've returned many of them to active duty."

"But the dancing energy inside of me. What is it?"

"That sensation you're feeling deep inside is your second death."

I didn't like the sound of that.

"37.9% of people end up here in Hell when they die. But 100% of the people who die in Hell, as you did a few hours ago, stay here after death. Even though you're dead, you can walk and talk and basically act like you're alive. You can exist here like that indefinitely. We've met folks here who died thousands of years ago."

Charles sagged in his chair.

"In other words, you're still *you*. But that little dab of energy within you gives you a way to truly die. If you focus on that little bit of light, and feed it with your mind and attention, it will grow and grow until it destroys you."

"It's a suicide option," Charles said. "I can sense that now."

"Kinda. It's more like an option to switch teams." The Major said. "When you take that option, your second death will consume you and turn you into a demon."

"That's where demons come from?" Karen interrupted. "Demons are just dead people who choose to die their second death?"

"You guys catch on quick!" the Major said brightly. Then he looked at his watch. "Third shift started an hour ago. Its bedtime. I'm going to show you guys to your tents. Try to get some sleep. Tomorrow is the first day of your new jobs! You're going to work in the City of the Dead!"

Chapter 4

Yummy, Nutritionally-Balanced Shakes

January 17th. First Shift

I bunked with Charles in a cramped tent that was nothing more than a lightweight tarp cleverly hung over a pair of cables strung between tall aluminum posts. Our beds were lightweight inflatable sleeping pads, and our blankets were thin, silvery sheets of mylar. Everything in Fort Kaizen was lightweight and easily compressed, rolled, or folded because literally every piece of gear had to be hand-carried across the river on the Boatman's boat.

Charles sobbed and wept for hours after I pulled my mylar blanket over me. I felt bad for him. After all, he died and was consigned to Hell. But I was utterly exhausted and I soon managed to ignore his sobs and fall asleep. Charles woke me up what felt like a moment later, needing someone to talk to.

"Jake, the Major said there were people who have been here for thousands of years."

"I know."

"Thousands of years, Jake. I don't think I can handle that." He sobbed for a few seconds. "That's a hundred times longer than I got to live on Earth. What kind of fucked up universe is this?"

I didn't know how to respond, but finally said "Maybe you'll feel better if you get some sleep."

"I *am* tired. Why? I'm fucking dead, Jake. Why am I *anything*? I shouldn't be tired or sad or anything at all. It's all wrong."

I fell asleep again, listening to Charles mumble his dark thoughts.

I woke to a recording of a bugle playing reveille. Ft. Kaizen, apparently, has a PA system. I sat up and pulled the cord to turn on the tent's light – a LED bulb zip-tied to one of the cables holding up the tarp. Charles was also sitting up in bed. Even for a dead person, he looked terrible. I doubted he had slept at all.

Major Williams flung the tent flap open and ducked inside. "Oh good, you're up. I thought you might not know that reveille means first call. You'd think it was the ice cream truck or something. Let's go grab breakfast."

Breakfast, and every other meal served in the dining facility, was a multivitamin, a glass of water, and a foil packet of powder to mix into the water to make a shake.

"Supplying this camp is a logistics nightmare." The Major continued his cheery narrative about Fort Kaizen as he

47

mixed his shake. "Everything has to come over on the boat. We're constrained by weight and volume. So, no solid food – just these yummy, nutritionally balanced shakes. Solid food is a luxury we can't afford. We need the logistics capacity for ammunition."

Now I knew why we were fed a high-calorie meal at intake – to prevent us from needing to eat, and consume valuable rations, as soon as we got to Fort Kaizen.

"Where does the water come from?" Karen asked, watching a glob of undissolved powder ooze off her spoon. Charles sat with us but didn't have a shake or a vitamin. The dead don't need to eat, so they don't get rations.

"The river," the Major answered casually. He tilted his cup back and drank his entire shake in one go.

Karen and I finished our shakes about ninety seconds later. The Major gave us a tour of Fort Kaizen on the way to the gate. It was a quick tour because Fort Kaizen isn't very big.

Fort Kaizen is a rectangle whose perimeter is a dry-stone, rubble-filled wall topped by concertina wire. The perimeter wall was clearly constructed from the grey rocks of the riverbank.

Three avenues (roads perpendicular to the river) intersect with four streets. Each of the blocks between the streets and avenues are filled with tents like the one Charles and I shared last night – tarps hung over cables strung between poles. Small portable generators sat on the ground in a few of the intersections, connected to electrical cables that ran to the lampposts, the PA system speakers, and into the tents.

"Here's the med unit," the Major said, gesturing to a collection of tents. "Weapons and ammo over there," he gestured to the opposite side of the avenue. "S-2 over there." The Major had forgotten that we didn't speak Army.

We passed a guard post – a crude dry-stone tower erected along the perimeter wall. A pair of soldiers stood on top – one wearing the same grey fatigues we were assigned at intake, the other wearing a union civil war uniform. The soldier in the modern uniform held a rifle. The civil war soldier wore night-vision goggles.

"Can I get a weapon?" Charles asked.

"Negative," the Major said. "First of all, you're civvies, so no toys for you. Second, you –" he turned and pointed at Charles " – are dead. The dead don't get weapons. It's too dangerous. Sooner or later, they'll try to fight their way back to the portal, and then the shit will really hit the fan."

We all brooded on the Major's words for two more of Fort Kaizen's short blocks. Then we found ourselves at the main gate on the side of the Fort opposite the river. The Major shouted to the guards on the tower to begin the exit protocol. We stood in front of the gate, waiting for the protocol to finish – we needed to know there were no demons nearby before we opened the gate. Pairs of living and dead soldiers manned a pair of stone watchtowers flanking the gate. The dead scanned the area for demons. The living held their weapons ready.

Our destination, the Major explained, was the City of the Dead. "Really more like the refugee camp of the dead. When the wandering dead stumble on the Fort, they don't want to leave. They love talking to the living. They love just being near the living. We're the most exciting thing that's ever happened in Hell. We can't have them just standing around outside the wire, potentially self-destructing into demons at any time. So we send them three kilometers away, to the camp. Most of our local hires live there and commute to the Fort."

An air horn sounded three blasts and the gate – a chain link fence topped with razor wire – rolled open. The landscape of Hell lay before us. A dusty, single-track trail wound away from the gate and was soon lost in the rugged terrain.

"No. I can't. I can't do it. I can't be here. Not forever!" Charles slowly backed away from the entrance.

"Okay, take a few deep breaths," the Major said.

"I don't need to fucking breathe! I'm fucking dead! I need the light."

"Charles, you just died yesterday. Give being dead a shot. It's not that bad."

"Don't do it!" one of the dead guards shouted from the tower.

"The light!" Charles shouted. He crumpled to the ground and screamed.

"He's doing it!" the dead guard shouted.

An alarm bell started ringing. The PA squawked, "gate response." There were shouts and people running through my peripheral vision. Charles writhed in pain on the ground, then fell still. Then he vanished.

Someone screamed "Biter!" The Major pushed me to the ground and drew his pistol. There were gunshots. A dozen or more. The Major's pistol sounded completely different from the rifles. I heard Karen grunt in pain.

More gunshots. More shouts of "Biter!" and "Demon!" Then "Cease Fire." Then it was silent.

Someone helped me back to my feet. Karen lay on the ground, a river of blood draining from her neck. A medic rushed to her and knelt to examine her wound.

"Don't bother," Karen said. Her voice was a raspy whisper. "I'm dead. You can't help me."

Everyone was still for a moment. The medic didn't move. "I said get away from me!" Karen screamed at her. "I'm dead, you can't do shit for me."

The medic stood and backed away. Karen rolled onto her knees, the motion spilling another pint of blood from her neck. She glared at the Major with black eyes. "You going to give me the speech about how my security clearance is still active?"

Major Williams didn't answer her. He ordered the gate closed, and had the guards re-run the exit protocol. They gave the all clear – Charles, or the demon he became, had left the area.

The air horn sounded again, and the gate rolled open. "Let's go," the Major said. He walked through the gate and dead Karen and still-living me followed him.

Chapter 5

The "City" Of the Dead

January 19th, second shift

My first visit to the City of the Dead (or the COD, as they call it at Ft. Kaizen) was the most depressing day hike I've ever been on. We walked there as a group. Me, Major Williams, and the recently-deceased Karen accompanied the second shift intel team and their security squad of living and dead active-duty troops.[1]

In total, we numbered eleven living and ten dead. The living soldiers were all young men who exhibited the mix of skilled professionalism and reckless youth that I rarely see outside of the military. The dead were also young, in the sense that they died while still under the age of thirty. But they were old too; they had been here for a long, long time. Three of them wore uniforms that looked to me as if they were from the first world war. Six looked as if they

---

[1] A note on the lingo here. They call this a "mixed casualty" unit because it contains non-casualty personnel (the living) and so-called "casualty" personnel (the dead). Mixed casualty units typically have a one-to-one casualty/non-casualty ratio.

died in Korea, or maybe Vietnam. One had a uniform with a dark blue shirt and light blue pants.

The dead soldier in the blue uniform saw me studying him. "Good morning, sir!"

"Oh, is it morning? I've kind-of lost track."

"Ha! There's no such thing as morning here," he said. "Or night or mid-day or anything else. I just always pretend it's morning. That way I always have the whole day to look forward to!"

"I always pretend it's Saturday," said his living partner. "Tyler" was stenciled onto his shirt.

One of the first-world-war guys joined the conversation. "That's a terrible idea – it means you're always working on the weekend."

"It means I always have something to complain about if I want to."

"I don't care what day or time it is," said the first-world-war casualty. "I just like to think that it's July."

"I like to think that every day is my birthday. And all of you jerks forgot about it again!" The Major said. "We're outside of the wire. Everyone shut up and pay attention."

After the Major's rebuke, we followed the dusty single-track trail in silence. A few hundred feet past the gate, the trail wound around the base of a low hill. We rounded the bend to be met with a nearly identical view – more single-track trail winding through the gravel and boulders. Now and then a cairn was placed on a boulder to show the way.

"Halt!" the Major shouted. "Dead eyes on the hills!"

On his order, the dead members of the security squad scrambled to the high-points of the surrounding terrain and scanned the surrounding area. Each of the dead eventually held their arms up – the all-clear sign – and the Major ordered us back into motion. We repeated this process every few hundred meters.

At our super-cautious patrol pace, it took nearly forty-five minutes to hike just two kilometers. Two kilometers of nothing but grey rocks and gravel and dust. The trail wound around the base of yet another grey hill, and suddenly we were on the outskirts of the city.

A throng of a few dozen people were gathered along the trail next to a small signpost. The sign – a piece of cardboard duct-taped to an aluminum post – was handwritten in black sharpie:

STOP

Living and Local-Hires Only Beyond This Point

Someone had crudely drawn a stop sign and a hand with an open palm below the words on the cardboard sign.

The group of men by the sign (there were no women) stood and formed a line as we approached. Nearly all of them wore some sort of military uniform.

Our three intel guys waved hello and approached the small group.

"These guys," the Major told Karen and I, "are US military. Or they were, anyway. We've selected them to be next in line for local hiring, when the slots open up. We've got them stationed here, keeping anyone from wandering down the trail to the fort. It's kind of like a job interview. If they screw up and let anyone pass, we'll hire someone else next time."

The intel guys had a short conversation with the throng of trail guardians, then reported back to the Major. "About a dozen people showed up here last shift. New folks, probably. In groups of three or four. None of them spoke any language our guys at the sign could recognize. They turned the new folks around and sent them to the city."

We left the group of prospective local-hires at the sign and walked another kilometer to the main part of the city.

To call the COD a city is even more of a stretch than calling Fort Kaizen a fort. There were no structures. No tents. No streets. Just a massive group of the dead sitting on rocks or wandering aimlessly through the bowl-shaped area nestled between a dozen low hills. It was the least organized, most depressing refugee camp I had ever seen.

"This is your refugee camp?"

"No," the Major answered with his usual exaggerated good cheer. "This is *your* refugee camp. We brought you down here to manage it."

"Is there any intake process at all? Do you know how many people are here?"

"New dead show up every shift. They either stumble into the camp by accident as they're wandering through Hell. Or they come in contact with a patrol or the fort and we send them here. My guess is there's a good seven thousand dead here right now."

I struggled to come up with what to say next. Too many thoughts struggled to be the next ones out of my mouth, The Major took my silence as the end of my need to talk to him. "Gotta find the last shift intel guys." He walked off.

"English! English!" Captain Marco, one of the intel guys who walked with us from the fort wandered into the crowd of the milling dead. "Anyone speak English?"

"What are you doing?" It was Karen. Her voice was still airy, as most of her breath came out of the hole Charles's demon form had gashed into her neck. I suppose she will sound like that forever.

"Gathering intelligence. I want to talk to someone who knows where the new people are."

"So, you just look for anyone who speaks English, and hope that they can somehow communicate well enough with everyone else to tell you what you need to know?"

"Pretty much."

"Well, that's bullshit." Karen stormed off.

"She is one grumpy dead person," Captain Marco said. Then he and his two other intel guys wandered away into the crowd, leaving me alone in the middle of the throng of dead. I began my own wandering, starting at the center of the area we called a city, and slowly spiraling out. I walked for hours, trying to get a sense of the place.

Unlike refugee camps of the living, the COD is occupied by people from literally every possible ethnic group and time period. I saw people dressed in Victorian-era clothes, a man wearing only a bear-skin, a woman in a hazmat suit, and more than a few people wearing kilts. The place would be a historian's dream, if we could afford to bring a historian down here, that is.

Many of the dead exhibited terrible wounds – the injuries that probably killed them. Most, though, were more-or-less intact, having died, I assume, from disease. Dead with faces covered in smallpox lesions were well represented. There were no children.

My semi-random wandering eventually brought me to Major Williams again. He was huddled with Captain Marco and the two other intel guys I hadn't met yet. He spotted me and waved me over.

"Tell me, mister Conner, what are your initial thoughts on your refugee operation here?"

"At first," I told the Major, "I thought it was a horribly run operation – nothing but a place where people are, well, *concentrated.*"

"Sounds hellish." Was making light of the fact I just suggested he was running a concentration camp built-into the Major's sense of humor, or does everyone get this way after a few months here?

"But then I realized a few things. The dead don't need to eat. And, other than being dead, they don't have medical issues. Food and health logistics aren't an issue here. Refugee operations are usually about keeping people alive until they can go back to wherever they came from. That mission doesn't make sense here. What *is* the point of this place?"

"First of all, the dead in this camp possess a trove of intelligence about Hell. They've wandered here for decades and centuries. Millennia even." He pointed at the guy in the bearskin. "We keep three shifts of intel here working twenty-four-seven. Talking to the locals and learning about the enemy."

"The enemy?"

"Satan. The Devil. Lucifer. The guy who brought his guitar from down here all the way to Georgia."

"I think it was a fiddle." I looked at Captain Marco. "This camp has provided actionable intelligence we can use to defeat the Devil?"

"Sorry. That's a high side conversation."

"You can't even tell me about the fiddle?"

Marco gave me an *oh please* kind of look. Or maybe it was a *I-hate-working-with-civilians* look.

"We'll handle the intel part," the Major said. "You have to deal with the second reason we need this magnificent sprawling metropolis."

"So, what's the other reason we need this place?"

"Here's the problem. At any time, any of these happy campers can decide that they're actually unhappy campers. They can choose to undergo their second death – to focus on the little light inside of them, blink out of existence, and be replaced by a demon, just like Charles. This city is essentially a group of thousands of time-bombs, each of whom could go off at any time. Your job is to keep them happy. Do not let them second-die. We literally do not have enough ammunition to deal with the demon-threat this camp can become."

I was about to respond with a military-esque "roger," but our conversation was interrupted by a vigorous, enthusiastic shout.

"Hello Major Williams!" The voice was male - deep and powerful. All of us turned to the source of the shout. A tall man with a fantastic beard and a fatal head-wound smiled at us. Karen stood next to him. A throng of two dozen more dead stood in a line behind them.

"Now you," Karen pointed to the next dead in line. A woman dressed in rags shouted. "Zdrasvootche! Mayor! Weeleems!" (That's what it sounded like to me anyway.)

60

"You!" Karen pointed at the dead man who was third in line. He smiled and shouted something that sounded like "Marhaben Alradydoo Williams."

Karen went down the line – each person shouted something in a different language. It took two full minutes for all of Karen's shouting-people to say their part. After the last person finally yelled something in a language that sounded to me like Japanese, Karen turned back to us, smiling. The terrible wound on her neck spread open like a second smile below the first.

It took Karen a moment to realize that our facial expressions indicated confusion and not amazement at whatever she had just done.

"I made Google translate, but out of dead people instead of computers."

Silence from me, the Major, and the intel guys.

"Alright," she said. "Let me explain. Say I want to talk to everyone here. Like, to tell them not to walk down the path to the fort, or … I don't know … ask everyone who showed up in the last shift to report to our intake area, not that we have an intake area."

She put her hand on the beard-guy's shoulder. "I tell Josephat what I want to announce. He shouts it in English." Karen took her hand off Josephat's shoulder and placed it on the shoulder of the next woman in line, "Vera here understands English and speaks Russian. She repeats what Josephat said, but in Russian. Then Suleman, who understands English also, shouts the same thing in Arabic. And we just go down the line. Not everyone understands English, but they understand at-least one of the languages up-the-line from them, and they repeat it in whatever-it-is that they speak. Swahili or medieval Korean or Ancient Navajo. Try it out." Karen ushered Josephat to the Major.

"It's Mister Conner's operation. Let's let him try out your invention." The Major gently turned Josephat to face me.

I leaned to Josephat and said "All newcomers report here."

Josephat put his hands on his hips and bellowed "ALL NEWCOMERS REPORT HERE." He really has a great voice. Vera shouted in Russian. Suleman shouted in Arabic, and so on for twenty more languages. I scrambled onto a boulder and looked around the city. Heads turned as the dead heard the announcement in their own language.

Soon a crowd of the newly-arrived dead formed next to the boulder I stood on. Captain Marco and the intel guys formed them into an orderly line and began interviewing them, one at a time.

January 22nd, second shift

I spend nearly all "day" in the COD – two shifts out of every three. Why not? All that's waiting for me back at the fort is a mylar blanket and a high-protein shake made out of water from the River Styx. Each day, Karen (who is now a permanent resident in the COD, thanks to her newly-deceased status) improves her translation system built out of dead people. She's recruited several hundred people into her system now. Some of them speak languages that haven't been spoken for millennia.

I spend my time talking to people in the COD. Thanks to Karen's work, I can speak with nearly everyone that I meet. Only a few folks, like the guy wearing nothing but a bearskin, seem to have unique languages, with no connection to any of the hundreds spoken by Karen's group of translators.

The dead tell me about what they've seen as they've wandered throughout Hell. They talk of cities of demons, of vast pits where armies of demons torture the dead ten-thousand at a time. They describe demons that stand as tall as skyscrapers, impossibly deep caves, mountains that rise a hundred miles high, and tribes of dead humans that live in peace with the demons. They tell me about the gates — a pair of closed doors the size of mountains, built into a wall that stretches to the black sky. It's impossible to say what is made up, what is exaggerated, and what is true.

January 24th, second shift

There are people in the COD who helped build Machu Pichu, Angor Wat, and countless castles and cathedrals and temples. If I gave these ancient stoneworkers some tools, I thought, they could build stuff – buildings or roads or statues. It didn't even matter *what* they built, as long as it helped keep them happy. Happy enough to avoid turning demon, anyway.

I convinced the Major to give me a few tools – a pick, two shovels, and three steel rods. ("It cost fifteen hundred dollars' worth of silver to transport this across the river," the Major complained).

Half an hour into my shift, I was standing on a boulder, trying to explain to thousands of yammering and shouting corpses that all I had were six tools and they needed to share. Karen's translators relayed my words from English into dozens of languages, then from those languages into still more, and more again after that. Communicating was such a tedious, noisy process that it took me a minute to realize that the hubbub had turned to panic.

An empty circle formed in the center of the crowd as the dead rushed away from ... something. I panicked for a moment, thinking someone had gone demon. It wasn't a demon, though – something visible was in the center of the expanding hole in the crowd. It was a pair of dead. An old man and another man who appeared to be middle aged.

The babble from the crowd made its reverse trek to me, translated from who-knows-what – medieval Bulgarian or Swahili or whatever – into who-knows-what-else and finally into scraps of English shouted by the translators.

"Son. Man and son. They are father and his son."

I finally understood. The pair of corpses in the center of the circle were a man and his son.

I borrowed a net radio from the security squad leader and contacted the Major. I asked why a father and son would produce such panic.

"Because they're a bloodline," he said. "If the demons find them, it's going to get real ugly."

"What should I do with this father and son?"

"Put them in your high-security area."

"I don't have a high-security area."

"Make one."

I got back on the boulder and explained to the crowd that I needed them to build a fortress.

Chapter 6

Bloodline

January 25th. first shift

The father and son who wandered into the COD didn't speak English. Karen helped me find a pair of translators who could translate from English to Urdu, and then from Urdu to the father and son's Punjabi. Through the translators, we learned that the two men had died simultaneously in a traffic accident in Pakistan about six months earlier. They crossed the river together, and somehow managed to survive this entire time while being mercilessly hunted by demons. The translators were uneasy being so close to a bloodline, and they wandered off shortly after I learned who the pair were.

I attempted to follow the Major's instructions to put the pair in a secure area by ushering them to a small rise in the center of the city. I had thought that the legions of the dead milling about the area would protect them from any demon activity.

When I arrived at first shift today, though, the Pakistanis had been forced out of the camp and were huddled at the base of a small hill on the perimeter. "The demons can smell them," I was told through interpreters of the dozen languages the crowd yammered at me. "We don't want them near us." I asked the Corporal who led the squad that accompanied the first shift's intel team to keep an eye on the two, then turned my attention to organizing the construction effort.

News of the fortress construction project traveled quickly throughout the city. A crowd of dead stoneworkers had gathered during my off-shift and managed to elect or nominate a leader – a man named Vasily. One of Karen's Russian translators was able to communicate with Vasily, but just barely.

"He speaks in a very old way," the translator explained. "Talking to him is like talking to Shakespeare."

The translator and Vasily had a long conversation involving a lot of hand gestures and blank looks exchanged between them. I assumed they were searching for common linguistic ground. Finally, the translator told me, "He built one of the towers of the Kremlin."

Vasily beamed at me. Then embarked on another long exchange with the translator. "I will build you a new Kremlin. Better even than the original!" he boasted through the translator.

Vasily was clearly a man with a plan. The other stoneworkers, representing nearly every stone-working culture in history, were enthusiastic despite the fact that hardly any of them knew what the Kremlin is. They seemed ready and willing to follow Vasily's orders.

Vasily had already selected a site for the new fortress. He led me to the top of the small hill in the center of the city. A few workers, all dead Russians, had already started clearing surface stones from the hilltop.

Vasily was explaining his plans for leveling the site when the roar of screaming crowds rose from below. From my position on the central hilltop, I saw a growing wave of chaos spreading across the camp. I followed the wave of panic backwards to its origin – the Pakistani father and son. I was able to make out one word of English from the hyper-lingual babble of the terrified crowd: *Demon*.

The security squad from Kaizen ran towards the Pakistanis. But they were at least 200 meters away, and had to muscle their way against the mob running the opposite direction. The father and son ran from their invisible (to me) attacker but were almost immediately cornered in a small gully. The son threw a rock, which stopped in mid-flight and fell to the ground.

The Pakistanis froze for a moment – transfixed by something I couldn't see. Then they *liquified*. It started with their arms – both arms of both men fell off their bodies and splashed onto the ground in a reddish-brown puddle. Then their legs burst like water balloons, and their bodies fell into the pool of their liquified limbs. For a horrible few seconds, they lay in the puddle, mouths agape, but seemingly unable to scream. Then their torsos melted away into the puddle.

In the description of the event that I got from the translators, the demon, a biter, knelt and drank up the puddle. Since the demon was invisible to me, I only saw the puddle that used to be the father and son rapidly vanish like water soaking into parched ground.

The squad from Kaizen broke through the crowd and opened fire – the returned-to-active-duty dead directing the living soldiers' aim.

Accounts of what happened next vary. The dead who witnessed the event all agree that the demon transformed upon drinking the remains of the Pakistanis. But beyond that, there is little agreement on the details. Some of the dead say the demon doubled in size. Others say it sprouted wings. Some claim the demon grew extra arms. Yet others describe new appendages like octopus tentacles. Something happened to its head, as well. Depending on who tells the story, it grew a new eye on its forehead, or a new mouth, or horns.

Fire from the squad eventually started hitting the invisible target. The newly transformed demon ran away from the camp. The security squad chased it for a short distance, but the demon was soon lost in the rugged landscape between the camp and the river.

Chapter 7

Do You Know What Our Mission Is, Mister Conner?

January 26th, third shift

I sneezed today in the dining facility. Everyone around me said "fuck you!" Why? Since praying in Hell attracts demons, nobody wants to risk saying "Bless You" when someone sneezes. So, they just shout "fuck you!" instead. Hilarious. Juvenile, but hilarious.

January 28th, second shift

One of today's new arrivals in the camp is an American who died recently. He said he was tortured by demons for over a month in some sort of machine that looked like a combination of a Ferris wheel and a rotisserie oven. I sent him along to the intel guys.

January 29th, third shift

I met Ft. Kaizen's commander today – Lt. Col. Hanson. He called me into his office (a rare triple width tent). I'd seen him around the base – a short, balding man with a perpetually serious expression. He seemed to have no interest in me. Until today.

The Colonel had his feet on his desk (really just a collapsible camping table). The Major sat next to him sipping a protein shake.

"Mister Conner, the Major tells me you're doing some interesting things in the COD."

"Yes, sir. I've put the dead to work building a secure area on the hill. They seem to enjoy the work, and the structure they finally create might have some utility."

"Great. Great." The Colonel put his feet on the ground and sat up straight.

"Do you know what our mission is, mister Conner?"

"Yes sir. We are invading Hell to neutralize Satan."

He looked at me over the tops of his glasses. "Invading. Really? I'm not so sure about that."

"We're a military force that came down here and started shooting at stuff. Isn't that, like, the definition of invading."

The Colonel rolled his eyes. "Running in and shooting a bunch of stuff is called a _raid_. An _invasion_ typically has the goal of conquering territory. It is debatable whether this," he gestured in a broad circle, "can be considered conquered territory."

Lt. Col. Hansen put his feet back onto his table. "Kaizen didn't use the term *invasion*. She called it Establishing a Permanent Supported Research Presence."

"Kaizen?"

"Doctor Kaizen. Doctor Helen Kaizen. The person for whom this fort is double-posthumously named. She was outside the vacuum chamber at Livermore when the original laboratory accident occurred. The accident that opened the first portal. It was Kaizen who figured out how to create a portal at will. Kaizen figured out how to stabilize and enlarge them too. She was the third person to enter a portal and the first to return alive. She was the first living person to cross the river. In both directions."

"Posthumously named? You mean she's dead? I can meet her here?"

"No. *Double*-posthumously. She died *twice*. Got killed by a demon on her seventh expedition here. Then she *went* demon. *On purpose.* She volunteered to be the subject of an experiment to test whether a method of halting a second death would function. It didn't."

"So..." I was still stuck on the fact we need to distinguish between posthumously and double-posthumously. "There's a demon running around out there that used to be Dr. Kaizen."

"Yep. Anyway, while she was alive, and also while she was just regular-dead, she strongly opposed the militarization of the project. But costs skyrocketed, the program gained a lot of visibility, a lot more people got involved. Then Kaizen went demon and a new policy was hammered out: Neutralize the Devil."

I tried to imagine a group of scientists entering the portal without having any idea what they would find on the other side. At least when I arrived in Hell, there was a big green-and-white sign telling me what to do. Did Kaizen and her team have any idea where they were? What happened when they met the boatman? What did they do when they encountered their first dead person?

"Who came up with the idea of a mission to kill the devil?"

"Neutralize. We're not sure if the notion of death can be applied to a supernatural being such as Satan."

"What I mean is, there's so many *other* things we could also do down here. We could learn about history from the dead. Or use them to answer questions about unsolved crimes. We could, I don't know, dump toxic waste here so it doesn't pollute Earth."

Hanson laughed. "The formulation of policy regarding the national interest with respect to Hell is far above my paygrade. I just get the extremely straightforward and simple mission of finding and neutralizing Satan. Do you know what the most challenging part of this mission is?"

"Uh…we don't know where Satan is?"

"Nope. That's a problem, obviously, but it's not the biggest problem. The biggest problem is supply. You see, I've got what is *literally* the worst supply chain problem in all of military history. Every person and every ounce of gear has to be hand carried across the river on the boat. On that small, shitty boat pushed along by that ancient slow-moving freak. Forty-eight grams of silver for each hand-carried load of supplies."

He turned to the Major.

"How many round trips did we manage today?"

"We had a good day with the boatman sir. We managed five trips. That's almost eight hundred pounds of supplies."

The Colonel turned back to me. "Eight hundred pounds a day. Maximum. For a unit this size. You know what our highest-weight supply item is?"

"Bullets?" I guessed.

"Diesel. For the generators. The radios, the lights, the *one* laptop that the intelligence fusion cell uses. We have to fill the tanks on the generators every four shifts."

"Why not send a boat through the portal. An inflatable raft or a small motorboat?"

The Colonel again gave me an over-the-top-of-his-glasses look. "You think we haven't tried that? We've brought boats through the portal. Drones too. We even brought a helicopter through the portal. You know what happens when we send them over the river?"

I didn't.

"They vanish. Poof. Gone. The only things that make it across the river are the boatman, his boat, and anyone who paid for the crossing."

The Colonel stood and paced behind his desk before speaking again.

"I have come to realize that, due to this supply chain challenge, I cannot command this operation as if it were a standard invasion. Doing so would put us right at the top of the list of military ass-whoopings, right under Napoleon's invasion of Russia, Little Bighorn, and the British at Isandlwana. A large component of the fuckery in all of these famous fuck-ups was a very limited and extended supply chain."

I didn't know why I was getting this speech. "Sir, I work in humanitarian aid –"

"I've found a different military pattern to follow. A more successful one. Do you know what my new model of success is?"

Again, I didn't.

"The conquistadores. They sailed across the ocean on wooden ships, *burned* them when they arrived in the New

World, and conquered a continent using whatever and whoever they found there. That's what we are going to do."

He unrolled a map onto his desk.

"You met a dead American yesterday. He reported that was tortured in some kind of metal oven mechanism."

"Yes, I remember him. I sent him to the intel team."

"He described the location where he was tortured. We have determined that the device in which he was cooked is in a cave in grid A079R16." He put his finger on the map, presumably in grid cell A079R16. "That's only sixteen kilometers from here. The device is metal. And there's fire. We can use both these resources. I'm particularly interested in the fire. I would like to use it to generate electricity with a boiler."

"Good idea, sir."

"Not really. But it's *an* idea, at least. I'm putting you in charge of it. First shift, you will accompany the Major and his assault team to this grid cell." He jabbed his finger on the map again. "Once the area is secure, you will oversee construction of a power plant."

I looked to the Major for help. "I'm not sure that I'm the right–"

"I'd love to be able to tell you that I chose you for this task because you're smart and capable and show a lot of promise. But really, it's because you're on this side of the river, and I don't have anybody else free right now."

The Major gave me a "hey – it's orders" kind of look.

"Cheer up everyone," Colonel Hanson said, brightly. "We're finally going to do something that's covered by the Army Field Manuals. We are going to seize and occupy an enemy position."

Chapter 8

The Wheel

January 30th, first shift

We left the Fort at the start of first shift. We were a mixed-casualty task force comprised of ten living personnel and twenty-three dead. The Major said this was the largest combat unit to ever leave Ft. Kaizen. Our orders were simple: Find the torture device in grid A079R16. If possible, disperse any demons and establish a defensive position inside the space. If that didn't prove possible, then gather intel and retreat back to Ft. Kaizen.

It sounds so stupid now, but I must admit – I *enjoyed* the three-hour hike to A079R16. The terrain was spectacular – without the moisture and dust of Earth's atmosphere, the view was incredible. The hills near the Fort blocked the view of the land farther from the river. When we reached the top of the first hill, I saw the true nature of Hell's landscape.

The jagged peaks of Hell's mountains pushed themselves into the sky, thrust upwards through some unimaginable, un-Earthly geologic process. Each peak was a Matterhorn or a Half Dome, with enormous overhangs lurching into space, impossibly sharp peaks, ridges like the back of Godzilla, and miles-high sheer drops. The mountains marched off into eternity.

Even though this was a military operation, I still felt the thrill of discovery. *Nobody* had been where we were going. *Nobody* had seen the things we were going to see. Nobody alive, anyway.

Militarily, the march to A079R16 was almost completely unremarkable. Two hours out from Ft. Kaizen, dead Corporal R. (died in the Korean war) spotted a burner about two kilometers away. We hit the ground and waited while the corporal squinted into the distance. He finally reported that the demon continued on its course away from us. We continued our march.

An hour later, the Major ordered us to stop and position ourselves in a small gully. We had just crossed into grid cell A079R16. The Major matched three living soldiers with three dead and distributed radios to each pair. He gave a short admonishment about the difficulty and cost of charging their batteries in our resource-starved operational environment and urged them to broadcast sparingly. Then he sent the scouting units out in different directions.

One of the units reported back ten minutes later – they had found a cave entrance that matched the dead American's description on the side of the hill next to the gulley. The Major ordered the scouts to return. He paired six living soldiers with twelve dead and sent them up the hill towards the cave entrance. The rest of us followed one hundred meters behind.

I watched the soldiers advance into the tunnel. They moved cautiously, the dead soldiers entering first to spot demon activity. After five minutes of tense waiting, the Major's radio squawked - no demons found in the cave, but we "*had* to get our asses up here to see this."

Me, the Major, and the rest of the unit scrambled out of the gully and quickly made our way up the hill into the cave. I'm not a geologist, and even if I was, my knowledge of Earth's geologic forces probably wouldn't be of use here, but the cave entrance didn't look like a natural feature to me. It looked like it had been carved into the hill.

The short tunnel opened into a large, high-vaulted space. The cave was well lit by huge tongues of orange and yellow flame that blasted out of a pit in the center of the floor. But the main feature of the chamber was a massive metal wheel that slowly turned over the flame. Like a Ferris wheel, this wheel had compartments along the perimeter for people. Unlike a Ferris wheel at a fair, the compartments on this wheel were small cages, each just large enough for one person. As the wheel slowly turned, the cages at the bottom were blasted by the flames. The metal was red-hot when it emerged from the fire and began climbing up and around the great wheel.

The torture wheel was filled to capacity with the dead. The corpses in the upper half of the wheel screamed at us to free them. The dead in the lower cages simply screamed incoherently from the pain inflicted by the fire. The dead trapped in the wheel were just as diverse as the dead in the city. Instead of hearing dozens of languages, though, their screams sounded all the same – the universal sound of humans in terror and agony.

Openings to five tunnels led out of the chamber, deeper into the hillside. The advance team had posted living/dead pairs to guard each tunnel. They knelt in front of each entrance, the living pointing their weapons into the black corridors. Their dead partners peered into the darkness.

"Well, I'll be danged," the Major said, gaping up at the wheel, "Look at all that metal. Where do you think it came from? What kind of metal is it?"

"What's being burned to make those flames?" a dead corporal wondered aloud.

"Shouldn't we try to free these people?" I asked.

The Major ambled closer to the fire pit, inspecting the mechanism that made the wheel turn. "It looks like some kind of Stirling engine, powered by the flames," he said.

The wheel was large enough to hold sixty people in cages around its edge. Their individual screams blended into a gruesome white noise – a cacophony of desperation and pain. But one of the voices stood out. A desperate female voice was shouting in English. I walked closer to the descending side of the wheel and listened, scanning the faces of the dead as they rotated past. The voice screamed again "Dad! Dad! Help me!"

The wheel made another quarter turn and Cara, my daughter — grey faced, black-eyed, and locked into a cage on the wheel's perimeter — rotated into view.

"Cara!" I didn't know what else to do other than scream her name. My daughter was dead. Dead and being tortured in the flames of Hell.

Chapter 9

Fall Back

January 30th, first shift

"Dad! Hurry!" The wheel pulled Cara, my beautiful daughter, lower and lower, towards the fire. I ran as close as I could to the base of the wheel. The heat from the flames was unbearable. The dead in the cages below Cara's were reaching out to me, screaming as the wheel pushed them into the fire. I leaned over the pit and touched Cara's hand.

The Major yanked me back from the edge of the pit. "Do not say her name! She cannot call you father! You two are a bloodline! Do you understand what happens when the demons find a bloodline?"

Cara's cage plunged into the fire and her cries became unintelligible. I shook off the Major's hands and ran to the ascending side of the wheel. Cara emerged, her face distorted from pain. The bars of her cage glowed a soft orange. "We're going to get you out of there. Just don't use my name. Don't call me dad."

She nodded her understanding as she rotated up the ascending side of the wheel.

"Demon!" One of the dead soldiers guarding an exit tunnel shouted the alarm.

"Burner!" The shout came from another tunnel.

Bursts of gunfire. Shouts from the other tunnels. More gunfire – within seconds of the first alarm each of the teams guarding a tunnel entrance was engaged. The remaining living soldiers ran to the tunnel entrances and poured more fire into the darkness.

"It's a trap!" the Major shouted. "Fall back!"

I screamed at him and pointed at the wheel. "I'm not leaving without her!"

The Major punched me in the face, knocking me down. He shouted "drag him out of here!" and a moment later strong arms grabbed me under my shoulders and hauled me towards the exit. Cara reached the top of the wheel and began her descent back into the flames, screaming for me to help her.

I tried to fight the pair of soldiers who hauled me out of the cave. I screamed that I needed to help my daughter. I tried to dig my feet into the ground to stop them. But they were young, and strong, and full of adrenaline from the demon ambush.

They hauled me down the hillside, all the way to the gulley where the unit was regrouping. I stopped struggling and they released me. I immediately started to run back to the cave, but was tackled and pinned to the ground by at least three men.

The Major shouted an uninterrupted stream of orders. He placed fire teams at the top of the gulley, ordered a SITREP to be radioed the Fort, told everyone to empty everything but ammunition from their packs, and sent dead scouts to hilltop positions along the route back to the fort. We were retreating. Retreating while my daughter still burned.

I screamed at the men holding me down, and screamed at the Major to go back and free the dead who were locked in the wheel. I called him a coward for retreating. I called him a sadist and a war criminal for letting the dead burn in the cave. He ignored me for a minute or two. Then he grabbed a rifle from one of the living soldiers and smashed the butt into my face.

I shut up after the Major broke my nose. My silence wasn't from the pain, though. Or from the threat of additional violence from the Major or his men. The blow gave me the clarity of mind to think of Lara. I thought of my wife, grieving for Cara, unable to contact me. Not even knowing whether I knew our daughter had died. Lara was alone, in the worst moment of her life.

If I retreated back to the Fort with the Major and the rest of the unit, I reasoned, I could apply for a hardship waiver, and possibly leave post early. But even if I could evac from this post to be with Lara, that still left Cara burning endlessly in the wheel.

One of the dead spotters reported a burner milling around in the entranceway to the cave. His live buddy fired a burst. "Missed. Too high," the dead spotter said. Another burst and another miss. The demon wandered back into the cave.

Lara. Lara my love. What kind of life will we have, knowing that our daughter is in Hell? How can I ever face you without having done everything possible to free Cara from the wheel?

The Major continued giving orders, preparing the unit for a withdrawal. He set up fields of fire, defined maneuver routes for disengaging squads, gave orders for contingencies and follow-on actions. The business of combat wasn't guts-and-glory. The business of combat was rapidly solving a series of complex technical problems. The Major was a master technician, dispassionately using every resource he had to support the retreat. Leaving most of our gear behind to increase our overland speed. Putting individual soldiers at high risk on scouting details to increase the unit's overall chance of success. Even smashing my nose with the butt of the rifle wasn't personal. It was just something he saw as necessary to maintain positive control of the unit.

I needed to think like him. Emotionless calculation, not the desperation of grief, was what I required. The demons surrounded the wheel. I needed to be in the cave, with the demons out of the cave. That was my problem. A problem I needed to solve *right now*.

This problem wouldn't exist if the soldiers with the weapons could *see* their targets. That was the root of it – the rules preventing the dead from using firearms. The dead servicemen would never break this rule – they were simply too good at being soldiers. But *I* could break that rule.

Emotions flooded back into my mind. Even though there was no longer any mystery about what would happen to me, the fear of death was still overwhelming. Worse than my own death though, was the fact I'd never see Lara again. My suicide would effectively be the murder of her husband, at a time when she needed me the most.

No. I had to think like The Major. Do what needs to be done whether I like it or not. Whether Lara would like it or not.

I stayed on the ground. I moaned and rolled around to continue to give the impression that I was no longer a distraction or a threat to the unit. I was soon rewarded with my chance. Sergeant Mullins rested his rifle against a boulder while he used the SINGARS to radio the Fort. I rolled to my feet and sprinted behind him, grabbing his rifle and pack.

The element of surprise – until then I was just an annoyance and not a threat – bought me all of three seconds. I scrambled out of the gulley, rolling over the top just before The Major unloaded his sidearm into the dirt and gravel behind me.

Later, I realized that rolling down the lip of the gully to avoid the Major's shots was pointless. My own death was key to my plan. I could have saved ammunition by letting the Major kill me himself. But at that moment, the passions and confusion of life still controlled me.

I scrambled up the hill, zig-zagging in an attempt to avoid fire from the gulley. But none came. Whatever logic the Major employed to determine how best to deal with me concluded that I didn't need to be shot on my way to the cave.

I dove into the cave entrance. The wheel continued its fiery rotation inside. The dead still screamed in pain. I couldn't hear Cara but I knew that her voice contributed to the howl of their screams. Without allowing myself any time to think about what I was about to do, I turned the rifle towards my chest and pushed the trigger with my thumb.

Nothing happened.

I had only ever fired a gun during counter-threat training. That was five years ago. And the gun I trained with was a regular hunting rifle, not a military weapon. The M16 has a lot of … I don't know what to call them … doohickeys. Levers and buttons and sliders to pull on. I slapped my hand on a lever on the side of the weapon, turned it back towards my chest and pushed the trigger. The last instant of my life was a flash. I didn't survive long enough to experience my fall onto the cave floor.

Chapter 10

The Sensation of Death

January 30th, first shift

My life force shrunk into nothing. For a moment, like the instant a ball hangs at the top of its arc, I simply didn't exist. Then I was dead. A little light appeared inside of me, just as Charles described it. A little sensation of light and life, dancing and urging me to focus on it.

There was no more to it than that. If the meaning of life can be found in the sensation of death, then life is meaningless. It was a simple transition, like that of wakefulness to sleep, or from joy to suffering. The intangible sensation of being alive was gone – I hadn't even known it was there until I experienced its absence. But everything else remained – my thoughts, my memories, my fear, my grief. There is no such thing as resting in peace. Death is just an actuarial trick of the universe, arbitrarily separating humans into the living and dead. Dying was just the universe's administrative bookkeeping, moving my name to the other side of the ledger.

Well, there was at least one major difference between being alive and dead. I could see the demons. They blinked into my vision like a bad special effect in a low budget horror movie. Burners and biters, just like in Mrs. B.'s paintings, stood in the cave, staring at me.

The demons exchanged looks with each other – a human-like gesture that was terrifying to see in these monsters. The look they exchanged seemed to say "are you *seeing* this guy?" It spoke to their intelligence. To their social structures. To what they were capable of doing as a group.

I put the stock of my stolen rifle to my shoulder. I closed one eye and lined up the barrel on the nearest demon – a biter with lethally-sharp, eight-inch claws and the sad face of an overweight, middle-aged man. I pulled the trigger. I was rewarded with an explosion from the muzzle and a demon writhing on the floor in agony.

I aimed at the next nearest demon. A ten-foot-tall burning humanoid figure. I aimed at its chest and pulled the trigger. My aim was off but I was lucky. I hit the demon in its face. It collapsed to the ground, squirming and writhing like it was having a seizure.

The demons didn't die when they were shot. Do they ever die? Can they be killed? I have no idea. But they sure don't like absorbing bullets. I methodically rotated through one hundred eighty degrees, putting bullets into every demon that entered my field of view. The M16 is an amazing machine – once I managed to make bullets come out of it, I couldn't miss. Like the biter and the burner that were my first targets, the rest of demons dropped to the ground and writhed in pain when hit.

Was it beginner's luck? Was I the Mozart of shooting demons? I'll probably never know. When the gun finally stopped working (out of ammunition, I assume), all the demons were on the ground. I pulled at the clip, trying to take it out to reload. It didn't come out. I wasn't going to figure out how to reload the weapon anytime soon, so I left it on the floor by the entrance and ran to the wheel.

The mechanism driving the wheel was a mechanical maze of interlocking gears, shafts, levers, and linkages. I had no idea how long the demons would be incapacitated. If I had a good four hours to spare, I'm sure I could have figured out the fundamental mechanical principles behind the mechanism of the torture wheel. But for all I knew, I had minutes, or even just seconds to free Cara.

I pulled on levers at random. Some didn't budge. Some moved smoothly but appeared to have no effect on the wheel. The dead were screaming at me – pleading for rescue and pointing at the machinery and shouting in languages I'd never even heard spoken.

"Dad – pull the short lever!" It was Cara. She had just emerged from the flames, trapped in a cage of red-hot metal. Her voice wavered – she was struggling to stay calm. I pulled at a small lever. Nothing happened. "No, the near one!" she shouted.

I tugged on another short lever and it moved with a high-pitched squeal. Its rotation caused a shaft to slide, which in turn operated more mechanisms next to the wheel. Like a chain of dominoes, the cages on the perimeter of the wheel fell open in a clockwise sequence. The dead spilled out, jumping from the wheel without regard to where they would land. Even falling headfirst onto the gears and levers was preferable to staying in the wheel.

Cara jumped from her cage at the top of the wheel, landing violently on the stone floor next to the fire pit. I ran to her and helped her up – she was dazed and clutched her hip. I grabbed her by the arm and ran to the exit, dodging the demons that still lay on the floor of the cave.

The dead from the cave, all sixty-one of us, teemed into the gully. The Major shouted at us, shouted at his men, and glared at me with a complicated look that seemed to communicate fury at my insubordination and respect for what I accomplished. More shouted orders and we were on the run again – all of us – back to Ft. Kaizen.

February 9th, first shift

Cara was killed in a car crash three days after I left for Aberdeen Proving Ground. She remembers waiting at a red light to cross Route 9. The light turned green, she started across the intersection, and then she was in Hell. She met the Boatman and crossed the river less than 72 hours after I did.

Hell works in complicated ways – Cara never saw the portal exit from the boulder, or the supply camp. The Boatman delivered her to a desolate spot on the far side of the river. She was captured by demons a few hours later and taken straight to the wheel.

The Major's assault unit and all of the dead I rescued from the wheel made it back to the Fort without further incident. The Major gave me his standard speech about my security clearance and my continued employment with the government both remaining active even though I was dead. Then I was sent to live in the COD with the rest of the refugees.

Even though I'm dead, the refugees in the COD still treat me like I'm in charge. It's like I'm the mayor of a graveyard. I meet with the Major every few days to discuss issues about management of the city, and to request additional supplies. So far, I've acquired two broken screwdrivers, three old issues of National Geographic that had somehow made it to the Fort, and one shovel.

We're still building the fortress on the hill in the center of camp. The dead like me – people who don't know anything about masonry – share the handful of tools we have. The dead with stone working skills direct our efforts. We've already built about eight meters of the wall that will eventually be the keep in the center of our fortress.

Chapter 11

Letter to Lara

February 15th, third shift

Lara, my love – I've found a way to get this journal to you. It's risky, though. I'm not going to write down any details of how it's being smuggled back through the portal to protect the people that are helping me.

Something is always the worst thing in your life. No matter how healthy or rich or lucky you are – no matter how much better off you are than so many others – there's always some small problem or unmet desire that can grow into the focus of desperation and anguish. Whatever this "worst problem" is, no matter how minor it would seem to people who are truly suffering, its importance will grow until it fills your mind if you let it.

For me, this problem was our finances. I let my worries about our financial problems grow into obsessions. So many things piled up at once – the mortgage, Cara's tuition, your medical leave. Maybe if I was a better person then the suffering and loss I saw in Haiti and Jordan, and in Indonesia after the tsunami, would have given me a sense of perspective. I have a sense of perspective now, far too late for it to matter.

Looking back, I see that we could have somehow gotten by without me taking on the risks involved in this post. We could have sold the house. Or asked your parents for help. I let my pride get in the way of reasonable solutions to our money problems.

The worst thing in my life now is knowing that I'll never see you again, and that I can't be with you as you grieve for Cara. These are the truly important things that now consume me, and I can't understand how something as trivial as a downturn in our finances once seemed so important.

My love, you've lost your husband and your daughter. If my journal makes it to you, at least you'll know that Cara and I are together and that we never stop thinking of you. Please find a way to be happy again.

Love,

Jake

The End

Printed in Great Britain
by Amazon

23781481R00056